The Adventures of Barthalamew the Nearsighted Dragon

Darlene and Krystal Johnson

iUniverse, Inc.

New York   Bloomington

iUniverse books may be ordered through booksellers or by contacting:

iUniverse
1663 Liberty Drive
Bloomington, IN 47403
www.iuniverse.com
1-800-Authors (1-800-288-4677)

ISBN: 978-1-4401-4738-8 (sc)
ISBN: 978-1-4401-4739-5 (ebook)

Printed in the United States of America

iUniverse rev. date: 05/12/2009

Dedicated to my son Michael, daughter Krystal and to all the children I have known and will know. A special thanks to my husband Byron, who came up with parts of this book. He is also my funding for this book.

The Dragon and the Spindle

Many years ago on a fine afternoon, on a rock by the edge of a deep, dark, dense forest, on the edge of Kalazara, was princess Charity. She is the eight year old daughter of King Fredrick and Queen Isabella. Princess Charity has long blonde hair that hangs in ringlet around her face, blue eyes and a very pretty smile. She is the finest spinner in the kingdom. She enjoys sitting on her favorite stone, spinning wool and watching the birds whenever she gets a chance.

One afternoon Charity went to her favorite spot, a large gray stone, shaped like a chair, it was bordered on one side by the deep, dark, dense forest and on the other a little way down is the kingdom of Kalazara. From here she can see the large gray castle and all the houses and tents in the kingdom. Charity watches and sees people moving among the buildings. This particular afternoon one of princess Charity's, eight year old friends, Prince Theodore came by and asked," Would you like to go exploring with me?" Prince Theodore is a very handsome eight year old boy. He is tall and thin, with dark brown hair and brown eyes.

" I suppose that I could go for a little while." said Charity putting down her spindle. So Prince Theodore and Princess Charity started on their way. After awhile they came upon a very scary looking cave.

Princess Charity said," We shouldn't go in something could happen to us."

Prince Theodore said," Nothing will happen if we go in for a little while."

Soon they entered the cave and were weaving around in the passages.

Meanwhile Queen Isabella and King Fredrick were worrying about Princess Charity. So King Fredrick and Queen Isabella sent out some of the knights to look for her. When they returned to the castle and reported to the King and Queen.

Meanwhile Princess Charity and Prince Theodore were still weaving through the passages in the cave. Finally they stopped to rest and Princess Charity said," We are lost and we will never find our way home." and she started to cry.

Prince Theodore said," Don't cry we will find our way home again." Then he put his arm around her to comfort her. Finally they settled in for a long restless night. Meanwhile in a different tunnel of the cave there is a dragon named, Barthalamew, who went for a walk in the dark, dense forest and he stumbled upon the rock where Princess Charity would sit and spin wool and watch the birds, this because he doesn't see very well. He picked up the spindle and the wool and took it back to the cave with him. He tried to spin but it wouldn't work so he went to sleep.

At the castle King Fredrick and Queen Isabella had just settled in for their long restless night. Soon all was quiet. They were worried about Princess Charity and they couldn't sleep. The King went to Charity's room and looked in hoping that Charity was there. It was very dark in the room. Strait ahead of the King was the bed, to the right of

The bed was the nightstand and a chair. On the left was the vanity and a dresser.

The next morning at the cave, Princess Charity and Prince Theodore woke up and started trying to find their way out of the cave. Barthalamew went looking for something to eat. Suddenly he stumbled upon the tunnel where the children were at, startled by his discovery, he dropped the spindle and accidentally stepped on it breaking it.

The dragon said," Hi, Barthalamew is my name, can I help you find your way out of my fine cave?"

Prince Theodore said," We don't know this dragon, we can't trust him, he might try to hurt us."

Princess Charity said," All I want is to go home to my mother and father."

At the castle King Fredrick and Queen Isabella were getting ready to go look for Princess Charity. The King and Queen are walking through the forest in search of Princess Charity, they came to the rock where Princess

Charity would sit and there wasn't anything there so they went on.

Back at the cave Princess Charity and Prince Theodore were following the dragon out of the cave, when all of a sudden they got separated from the dragon and headed down the wrong tunnel and they became trapped by a cave in. Barthalamew came to rescue the children. He moved all the rocks and freed the children. Then he led the way again, they walked for a long time. Finally they came to the entrance to the cave. Then they went to the rock where Princess Charity would sit. So the dragon left the children there and went to find something to eat. Barthalamew felt badly about breaking the spindle that he went to find a present for the Princess. Barthalamew searched for a long time to find just the right gift for the Princess. When he found it, it was so spectacular and golden, it was a golden spindle. But that wasn't enough he wanted something more. So he searched some more and what was needed with a spindle but wool. So he found a hundred pounds of wool, and left three golden scales, then he took it back to his cave to keep it safe until nightfall so he could take it to the rock to surprise his new friend.

King Fredrick and Queen Isabella were still looking for Princess Charity and couldn't find her. Soon they were back in the woods and there was still no sign of the princess. After an hour they started back to the castle. On their way past the rock where the princess would sit, they saw the princess sitting there crying. " Why are you crying?" they asked.

The Princess answered," Someone has taken my spindle and wool."

The King and Queen said," We will get you another spindle and some more wool." So back to the castle they went. After they returned to the castle they talked about what happened.

Princess Charity said," Mother and Father, Prince Theodore and I will never do anything like this again without permission."

The next morning there was a big commotion in the kingdom. One of the King's bearers of bad tidings came and told the King that there was a large golden dragon coming toward the kingdom. The King called for his most loyal knight, Sir Currado. Sir Currado came to see what the king wanted and he explained what the problem was.   King Fredrick asked Sir Currado to fight the dragon, Barthalamew.

Meanwhile Barthalamew was slinking into the kingdom. The gentiles of the kingdom were throwing stones at the dragon, Barthalamew, as he passed, soon he was stumbling over stones. After an hour he was finally past the kingdom. Barthalamew came to the castle and stopped to look at it for a moment, finally he made it across the drawbridge into the courtyard, where he came face to face with Sir Currado, they stood and stared at each other for awhile. While this was happening, Princess Charity was in her room sitting at her window looking out over the courtyard, she sees Barthalamew and Sir Currado standing together. Princess Charity ran down the stairs and into the courtyard, she was yelling," Don't kill this dragon, he saved my life. Don't hurt my friend Barthalamew the dragon." The dragon had a pouch that he wanted to give to the Princess. He handed the pouch to Princess Charity, she opened it and saw a golden spindle. After that Barthalamew had Princess Charity follow him to the forest and there by the rock was a hundred pounds of wools. Princess Charity was so excited that she ran all the way back to the castle to tell her mother and father about the wool and spindle, that the dragon had given her. The King and Queen were very surprise to realize that their daughter had made friends with a dragon. That evening Princess Charity told the King and Queen that she had made friends with the dragon because he saved her life.

The Queen invited Barthalamew to have supper with the family, Barthalamew stayed for supper and he had a very tasty meal of fresh meat and vegetables. After the meal the King sent Sir Currado and another knight to bring the wool to the castle. The King and Queen invited Barthalamew to come live at the castle with the family. Barthalamew declined the offer and stayed at his very fine, cozy cave. Charity went to her room and got the spindle and some of the wool, then went to the parlor and started to spin. Princess Charity decided to make a blanket for her new friend. After spinning some wool, she dyed it a bright golden color and some she left white, then she started to knit a very large and heavy blanket. They still became the very best of friends and lived happily from then on in the kingdom of Kalzara.

Barthalamew and the Golden Egg

One fine morning Barthalamew went for a walk in the forest when suddenly he stumbled upon a beautiful golden, magical egg that seemed to appear from nowhere, but the egg was left by a magic wizard. Not knowing what to do, he went to find his friend, Princess Charity. Barthalamew set out for the castle to get his friend. When Barthalamew gets to the castle, he found Princess Charity in the garden sitting quietly holding her spindle. Barthalamew was so excited about finding the egg, that he startled Princess Charity.

He asked," What is the matter with you on such a lovely day?"

Princess Charity answers," I want some adventure to fill these lovely days." So Barthalamew asked Princess Charity to go with him on an adventure. Soon they ran into Prince Theodore looking very bored, so they asked him to join them.

Prince Theodore said," Yes, I would like to join you, Princess Charity." Then they set off to se Barthalamew's new found treasure, when they arrived at the spot where the egg was they were surprised to see a golden egg. So Barthalamew asked what they should do with the egg. Princess Charity suggested that they the egg to the castle and ask mom and dad what to do with it. So Princess Charity and Prince Theodore carried the egg to the castle garden and laid it under the willow tree. Princess Charity ran to get her father, King Fredrick. He came to see what the trouble was. He said that they should build a warm nest for the egg. As the sky turned rosy pink, the children and Barthalamew hurried to make a warm nest for the egg. By the time they finished the nest, it was time for Prince Theodore to go home, so he left. Barthalamew on the other hand stayed to watch over the egg.

Princess Charity said," Barthalamew, you don't have to watch over the egg."

Barthalamew said," I need to make sure that nothing happens to it."

In the morning Princess Charity ran downstairs, out the door and to the egg, to her surprise Barthalamew was laying huddled around the egg. Charity walked quietly over and tapped Barthalamew's, cold, damp scales, to wake him. He woke with a start and asked Charity, " Why did you wake me like that?"

Princess Charity said," I wanted to make sure that you were alright after such a chilly night. How is the egg this morning?"

Barthalamew answered," The egg is very toasty and warm in it's nice warm nest." After completely checking the egg, Princess Charity invited Barthalamew to join her for breakfast.

Meanwhile in the deep, dark, dense forest the wizard, Bortommnis was searching frantically for the magical egg. He was moving rather rapidly through the forest. As he emerged from the forest he spotted the castle. Bortommnis hurried to the castle in hopes of finding the egg. Back at the castle Princess Charity was sitting near the egg spinning some wool, when all of a sudden her mother called her and Barthalamew to do something for her. While they were gone Bortommnis sneaked into the garden and took the egg and took off with it. When Princess Charity and Barthalamew returned to their surprise the egg was gone. Princess Charity started crying and said," Our beautiful, golden egg is gone forever."

Barthalamew said," We will get all the help we can to help us find the egg, so don't worry so much about it." As this was going on Prince Theodore was on his way to see Princess Charity and find out how the egg was. As he was walking through the forest he spotted a man with an egg that looked like, the new found egg that his friends had. So he followed the man as far as Barthalamew's cave. The man, Bortommnis went in the cave. Prince Theodore hurried on to the castle, where he found his very distraut friends.

Prince Theodore asked," What is wrong with my wonderful friends on this fine day?"

Princess Charity finally was able to stop crying long enough to answer," Our beautiful golden egg has disappeared, and we don't have any idea where to look for it."

Prince Theodore said," I just saw a man in the forest with a golden egg."

Princess Charity asked," Do you know where he went?"

Prince Theodore answered," Yes, I know where he went, get some help and follow me." Charity ran into the castle and got some of the knights and followed Prince Theodore to the cave. Soon they were at the entrance of the cave, Barthalamew said," We need to split up into three groups, Princess Charity can take four men with her, Prince Theodore can take four men with him, and I will take four men with me." So they all split into three groups and each took a path and started looking for the egg.

Meanwhile deeper in the cave wizard Bortommnis was trying to remember how to reverse the protection spell . In the tunnels the others were having no luck finding the egg. Barthalamew and his group finally stumbled upon wizard Bortommnis and the egg, Barthalamew said," Would you give me the egg and come with me to my friends castle."

Wizard Bortommnis said," No, you can not have this egg, it is my egg because I am the one that left it in the forest."

Barthalamew said, " I found this beautiful, golden egg and took care of it, so it is mine."

Wizard Bortommnis said," I am the one who created this egg, and I will not give it up." Finally Barthalamew suggested that they head back to the castle. So Sir Currado tied up the wizard and they headed for the entrance of the cave. Meanwhile the others decided that it was useless to try any longer to find the egg. So they headed back to the entrance. Soon everyone got to the entrance. When Barthalamew and his group got to the entrance, they, Barthalamew and Bortommnis were still arguing over the egg. Princess Carity suggested that they take the egg to the castle and let her father decide who's egg it is. Everyone agreed that would be the best idea. So they all went to the castle, as soon as they arrived at the castle, King Fredrick came running to the garden, because of all the noise. King Fredrick asked what all the comotion was all about. Princess Charity told him that Barthalamew and Bortommnis are arguing over the golden egg, would you please decide who's egg it is? Barthalamew put the egg in the nest and wizard Bortommnis started yelling and complaining because Barthalamew took care of the egg.

King Fredrick snorted," Enough is enough of this behavior and temper tantrums, I will decide in the morning who shall get the golden egg." So they locked wizard Bortommnis in the dungeon and posted a guard around the clock. Barthalamew stayed with the egg all night to make sure nothing would happen to it.

Soon morning came and everyone met in the garden to find out what the decision was. The King called everyone's attention and said," I have made my decision, Barthalamew will have the egg because he has been so loyal to the egg since he found it."

Wizard Bortommnis," It's not fair to me, I am the one that created this egg, I should be the one to get the egg."

King Fredrick said," Bortommnis, if you want to stay at this castle and try to get along with Barthalamew. You can help Barthalamew take care of the egg, under the strict direction of Princess Charity."

Wizard Bortommnis said," Well I suppose I can give it a try, but I can't garettee that I will be able to get along with that slimey, scaly dragon."

The King said," If you don't agree to my terms, you will be banished from my kingdom forever." So the wizard agreed to try, at the castle everyone tried to get along with each other. After a couple of months, Barthalamew was checking on the egg and it seemed to be moving. Barthalamew went and got Princess Charity to come and see what was going on. Princess Charity called her mom and dad to come see what was happening in the courtyard, wizard Bortommnis also came.

The egg was finally starting to hatch, as the egg started to crack, they heard a very loud pop, Barthalamew saw a very tiny blue tail coming out of the egg. Soon the baby dragon was finally here. Then everyone was happy because it was finally here, Barthalamew started finding fresh fish and meat for the baby dragon to eat. Princess Charity and Prince

Theodore started bathing the baby dragon and oiled his scales. Everyone was helping take care of the baby dragon, they named the baby dragon, Michael. Wizard Bortommnis was doing a very good job of helping care for Michael the dragon, under the watchful eye of Princess Charity. Everyone looked out for the baby dragon, Michael and they all loved the little fellow. From then on everybody cared for the dragon baby.

Barthalamew and the Baby Dragon

Four months after the baby dragon was born, Barthalamew started teaching the baby dragon some of the things he needs to know. Barthalamew and Michael, the magic dragon were becoming very close. Barthalamew kept catching fish and fresh meat for Michael to eat. Finally it was time to start teaching Micheal to hunt. In the meantime Princess Charity and Prince Theodore worked very hard everyday to help find food and bath and oil the baby dragon's scales. Also everyone was very helpful when it came to caring for Michael, except for Bortommnis, the wizard. So King Fredrick, banished him from the kingdom forever, because he refused to do any of the work with the baby dragon, Michael. Micheal was so very little and he was very hard to teach, he had a very short attention span. One day Michael, the magic dragon took off and went on an adventure all by himself. When Barthalamew went to get Michael, to his surprise he was gone, so Barthalamew went to find Princess Charity and told her, she started crying.

Princess Charity sobbed," Why has our fine little magical friend left our fine kingdom?"

Barthalamew said, in a comforting voice," I am sure he hasn't left forever."   Still sobbing she told him that she was afraid that he would get lost or hurt. " Could we go find him, please?" asked Charity.

Barthalamew said," I really think that he will come back on his own, give him till tomorrow and if he isn't back, we will see about going to look for him."

Princess Charity said," Alright then we will look for him tomorrow." By now the sky was turning some very beautiful shades of orange, red and pink. Michael the magic dragon, had certainly gotten himself lost. So he settled down for a long, scary, lonely night, when he settled down he realized all kinds of sounds, he never heard before.

Meanwhile back at the castle everyone was worried about the baby dragon, but everyone settled in for a long miserable night, especially Princess Charity because she was the closest to Michael the magic dragon. Bartholomew went to his cave and lay there thinking about his little friend. Barthalamew knew that Michael could be almost anywhere, finally he fell asleep. Soon it was morning and the sun was just coming up and Bathalamew woke and hurried to the castle, where he found Princess Charity sitting under the willow tree, by the nest crying uncontrollably. Barthalamew told her to go ask her father, King Fredrick, if they could go find Michael. King Fredrick told her, " Yes, you may go look for our fine little dragon, but be very careful because Wizard Bortommnis is out there and he is determined to get Michael for himself.

Princess Charity said," I will take Barthalamew and Prince Theodore with me." So Princess Charity and Barthalamew headed for the forest, on their journey they bumped into Prince Theodore, who was headed for the castle. Princess Charity asked Prince Theodore if he would like to join them. Prince Theodore answered, of course I will join you.

Meanwhile in another part of the forest, Michael the magic dragon, was finally waking up. " Oh my goodness! What are you doing here Bortommnis?" said Michael.

" I am here to take you home." said Bortommnis

" Oh boy, you are going to take me home!" exclaimed Michael. " That is right, Michael." said Bortommnis.

Meanwhile Princess Charity, Prince Theodore and Barthalamew were walking through the forest, when Princess Charity exclaimed, " Look, here are Michael's footprints in the dirt!"

Prince Theodore said, " Let's follow the tracks and maybe we will find him."

" Good idea, Prince Theodore." said Barthalamew.

Elsewhere in the forest Bortommnis was carrying Michael to his lair. Michael struggled to get away, while he was struggling to get away, he kicked Bortommnis and got away, but he was so lost that he stayed at

19

Darlene and Krystal Johnson

Bortommnis's lair, for awhile. At Barthalamew's cave, Princess Charity, Prince Theodore and Barthalamew were talking about how they could find Michael. Princess Charity started to sob," Where oh where can our fine little friend be."

Prince Theodore said," Why doesn't Barthalamew fly around for awhile to see if he can locate him."

" Great idea, would you ask him?" said Princess Charity.

Prince Theodore said," Barthalamew, would you please fly over the forest and see if you can spot Michael?"

Barthalamew answered," Of course I will fly over the forest and find Michael."

Back at Bortommnis' lair, he was trying to get Michael to use his powers, he wouldn't do what Bortommnis wanted him to.

Michael said," Bortommnis, you don't have a heart."

Bortommnis said," Why do you say I don't have a heart?"

Michael said," 'Cause of the way that you treat people."

Wizard Bortommnis said," Michael," Have a great, kind, beautiful heart." A puff of gray smoke and Wizard Bortommnis was good and kind.

In the air over the lair Barthalamew was fling, he lands outside of the lair's door. Meanwhile inside Wizard Bortommnis mixed a potion and rigged a trap for Barthalamew. As Barthalamew walked in, he was sprayed by the potion, To his surprise, Bortommnis and Michael were there together.

Barthalamew said," Oh my goodness, what was that liquid?"

Bortommnis said," This potion gives you magic powers."

Barthalamew said," Are you alright Michael?"

Michael answered," Yes, I am alright."

Barthalamew said," Another egg!"

Bortommnis said," Yes, another egg, it was made to be a companion for Michael."

Barthalamew said," Michael, let's go get Princess Charity and Prince Theodore and go home."

Michael said," I will not leave without my new friend, Bortommnis."

Barthalamew said," Ok, I suppose that he may come with us to the castle, but he has to prove that he can be trusted again and I don't know if King Fredrick will let him back into the kingdom." So they hopped on, Barthalamew takes off and Bortommnis has to steady the egg. Michael has to fly fast to keep up with Barthalamew.

At last they get to the cave and Princess Charity hugged Michael, the magic dragon. Michael and

Barthalamew used their magic to transport everyone to the castle.

King Fredrick said," I banished Bortommnis from this kingdom."

Michael protests," I want Bortommnis to stay, 'cause he saved me from the big, terrible, dark, dense forest."

King Fredrick said," Bortommnis, you are welcome to stay as long as you can be trusted."

Barthalamew said," What about the egg, Bortommnis?"

Bortommnis answered," The egg is hatching!"

The egg cracked and out came a little copper colored female dragon. Princess Charity names the little tyke, Marrissa. Everyone said," Isn't she a beautiful little dragon." Everyone agreed that Marrissa should stay with the family at the castle. So everyone lived at the castle and everyone helped care for all the dragons who lived in the kingdom.

Barthalamew Goes
to the Future

On this wonderful, bright, glorious day Barthalamew, Michael, Marrissa, Princess Charity and Prince Theodore were out exploring and enjoying an Autumn day. In the forest the leaves were turning shades of orange, yellow and red. As they were enjoying their adventure, back in the area of the castle, Bortommnis was devising a potion to try and get rid of Barthalamew once and for all. He wanted Barthalamew out of the way forever, as Barthalamew and the others were coming back they were walking through the forest enjoying their walk.

Back at the castle Bortommnis had his potion ready. After Barthalamew and everyone split up and went their own ways, Barthalamew headed for his cave, as he past Bortommnis, he was sprayed with the potion and soon Barthalamew found himself in a strange place. He was very scared and didn't know what to do. Barthalamew started wandering around this strange place. Soon he came upon a park with lots of trees, so he went into the trees and sat down to rest. After awhile, he woke up and heard all kinds of noise, he was startled and afraid to move.

Meanwhile back at the castle Princess Charity was sitting in the garden doing some spinning of wool and enjoying a beautiful, orange, yellow, red and pink sunset. When all of a sudden Michael and Marrissa came to the garden, the two little dragons were very excited and they wanted to tell Princess Charity about something that they found in the bushes. Princess Charity followed them to where they found this thing they wanted to show her. On the left was the garden wall and on the right as they walked was a line of bushes, in the bushes there was some kind of sprayer with a liquid in it.

Princess Charity said," Looks like something that Bortommnis would make."

Michael asked," What would that be used for?"

Marrissa said," Yeah, what would it be used for?"

Princess Charity said," I don't really know what it would be used for, I will have dad come and look at it in the morning." By this time it was getting dark, so Princess Charity and the two little dragons went back to the castle and had their supper.

Meanwhile in the future Barthalamew had decided that he would stay in the trees until daylight, so he settled down for the night. Soon it was daybreak and Barthalamew had started to look for something to eat, because he was so hungry. Soon he stumbled upon a small child named, Vincent. Barthalamew had startled the young boy, Barthalamew introduced himself to Vincent.

Vincent asked," What are you and where do you come from?"

Barthalamew answered as best he could," I am a dragon and I come from the past. Could you please help me find my way home, I am lonely for my friends."

Vincent being a smart child said," I will do all I can to help you get home, Barthalamew." So the conversation between the two went on for quite awhile. Finally Vincent said to Barthalamew, I have to go have my lunch now, I'll bring you something when I come back then we can figure out how to get you home. See you in a little while.

In the past at the castle Princess Charity was up and had already had her breakfast. Her father came down and he had no than got to the dining room door and she, was asking him to come to the garden and see what she found. He told her to let him have his breakfast first then he go see what was so important. After he finished eating, he went with Princess Charity to the garden and there in the bushes was the sprayer with the liquid in it.

Princess Charity asked," What would this be used for?"

King Fredrick answered," I believe that it is some kind of vanishing spray, Charity. This looks like some kind of Bortommnis' work, I will have to talk with him. Has anyone seen Barthalamew lately?"

Princess Charity said," Not since yesterday, and he was on his way to his cave."

Meanwhile in a house of the future, Vincent was trying very hard to tell his mother and brother and sister about the dragon, he found in the park. But they just said that he had a wonderful imagination, so when he finished his lunch, he grabbed some extra food and put it in a bag and took off for the park. When Vincent arrived, he called for Barthalamew. Barthalamew had been napping behind a big oak tree, Vincent gave Barthalamew the food and let him eat. While Barthalamew was eating, Vincent was talking about how they could get Barthalamew home. First he wanted to get Barthalamew some glasses, so he wouldn't have to stumble around.. So when Vincent left, he went to see a friend of his, the eye doctor. Vincent told Doctor Risen about the dragon's problem, and asked if Doctor Risen could help. Doctor Risen said," I will go to the park with you and see what I can do, but I can't promise anything." So Vincent went home and had his supper and bath and went to bed. Meanwhile under the oak tree, Barthalamew settled down for another night in this strange land.

At the castle Princess Charity was in the garden spinning some wool , when Michael and Marrissa came and asked if she would like to go for a walk. Princess Charity said," Not right now, I am to worried about Barthalamew to do anything, right now. So off went the two little dragons for their walk, soon it was time for supper and all Princess Charity did was pick at her food. Her mother was worried about her daughter, so she told Princess Charity to go on to bed, her mother, Queen Isabella, went up to see how her daughter was doing. Isabella found Princess Charity crying in bed and she asked," What is the problem, Charity?"

Princess Charity answered in sobs," W-Why is B-Bortommnis s-so set on getting rid of B-Barthalamew?"

Queen Isabella said in a comforting voice," He is probably jealous of Barthalamew, after all we do pay a lot of attention to Barthalamew."

Princess Charity said," B-But Barthalamew was here first and h-he should have a lot of attention." Queen Isabella told Princess Charity to try to sleep and that they would figure it out in the morning. The next morning Princess Charity woke early and went for a walk in the forest..

Meanwhile in the future Barthalamew was waking up. Vincent was up already and at Doctor Risen's place and ready to get going. Doctor Risen hurried to keep up with Vincent, when they got to the park Barthalamew got so scared he turned invisible.

Vincent said," Don't be scared he can help you see better and possibly help you to get back to your time." So Barthalamew turned visible again, the doctor checked everything, I think I have a solution at the office . So the doctor, told Vincent and Barthalamew, that he would be back in two hours time. Back at the office Doctor Risen made a special pair of glasses for Barthalamew, he also created a formula to send Barthalamew back to the past.

At the castle Princess Charity was sitting quietly under the willow tree. All of a sudden she was grabbed from behind, she hadn't realized what was happening. The capture was a dragon by the name of, Thaldar the evil, he took her back to a large desert place where it was very hot. Queen Isabella went to the garden to get Princess Charity and she was no where in sight.

In the park, Vincent and Barthalamew were playing games. Finally Doctor Risen came back. He had a large pair of glasses and a sprayer.

Vincent said," What is that for?"

Doctor Risen said," This is so our friend can go home."

Barthalamew put on the glasses and told the doctor thank you. Vincent started to look sad and Barthalamew felt sad too, so he gave Vincent a beautiful golden scale that had fallen off. Doctor Risen said," Are you ready, these are magic glasses all you do is think of this park and you can visit anytime."

Barthalamew said," Vincent, if you ever need me just look deep into the scale and call my name."

Doctor Risen sprayed Barthalamew and he disappeared and reappeared in his own time at the castle. Queen Isabella was there and she was very upset.

Barthalamew asked," What is wrong?"

Queen Isabella answered," Princess Charity has been kidnapped, can you find her and bring her back?"

Barthalamew said," Of course I will find her and bring her back." So off he went to see if he could find out where she was taken.

A Visit to Desert Dragonland

Barthalamew started on his way, because he was very worried about his friend. As Barthalamew started off, he saw something shining in the distance. He hurried over to see what it was, it was Charity's crown. So he headed that direction, he walked for several miles and realized that he was very hungry so he stopped for something to eat. After eating he decided to take a nap, so he lay down to rest. Barthalamew started dreaming, he dreamed of a wizard named, Galdar, and he told Barthalamew to go toward the tall grassy hill that looks like a wizard's head. I'll be with you whenever you need me. Finally Barthalamew woke up and started walking again. On his left he could see nothing but grass for as far as the eye could see. On the right there were trees as far as the eye could see. So on he went far, strait ahead was the hill that Galdar had told him about.

In large cave in the desert of Dragonland, Thaldar had Princess Charity and wouldn't let her go anywhere and the cave really smelled terrible. Princess Charity was really scared and was starting to get a little worried that she was going to be eaten by this fierce dragon. She was so scared that she was shaking. Zaldar came into the cave from the cave from the of where she was sitting. He was a very tall, skinny man, with a dark red gown, with a tall pointed hat. Princess Charity asked," What are you going to do with me?"

Zaladar answered ," I understand that there are three dragons that live with humans in your kingdom. I plan to hold you until I get them all."

On the plain where Barthalamew was he had traveled as far as he could go, so he decided to stop for the night. He lay there and watched the sky change from a gorgeous orange to a beautiful rosy pink. Barthalamew lay thinking about Wizard Galdar and what he told him. He was so busy thinking that soon started to doze off. Soon he was dreaming and this time his dream was more of a vision. He dreamed about Princess Charity and where she was. It scared him and he turned invisible, but he wasn't worried about it. Then Wizard Galdar appeared and told him," You need to control your powers, you need to use your invisibility when it is needed."

Galdar said," In the morning you must go over the hill of a wizard's head and walk for two more days to get to the desert."

At the cave in the desert, Princess Charity settled as best she could for some rest. Thaldar sat on guard all through the night, Zaldar was in his room in the cave. This room was very big, to the right was a large wall bookcase full of books, next was a large wooden desk. To the right of the desk is a large work area where there were lots of tubes, bottles and all kinds of liquids. Next was a four post canopy bed. To the left was a living area, on the first wall was a large fireplace, to the left of the fireplace was a large cupboard and a table and a chair. Left of the table and chair was living furniture and a few odds and ends, soon Zaldar settled in for the night.

Unknown to anyone the two little dragons took off, Michael and Marrissa were worried about their friends, so they slipped away and started to find out where their friends were. They walked for quite away and decided that they would rest for the night.

Finally it was morning and Barthalamew started on his quest again, he walked for a long way and decided to find something to eat. After eating he walked to the base of wizard hill and looked at it for a moment. While he was looking at the wizard hill, he decided that it would be easier to fly over it. So he flew over the hill and landed. He walked for several miles. Soon he lay down and took a nap for awhile, after he woke up he started on his way again.

In the desert cave Zaldar offered Princess Charity something to eat, she ate and told Zaldar that he would never get away with what you are doing. Zaldar was getting very nervous about what Princess Charity was saying. So he had Thaldar put a gag on her so she couldn't talk. Then Zaldar went to his room and tried to come up with a way to make the dragons forget their human friends.

Barthalamew walked on for a long while, he walked for several hours, the sky was turning rosy pink in color, so he decided he had better find something to eat. He ate a rabbit and then settled down for the night. As he slept, he dreamed of the long trip and still no sign of where Princess Charity was. Something startled Barthalamew and he turned invisible again. Soon he was dreaming, Galdar came to him again and he told Barthalamew that he had one more day to travel, you must travel across a desert to get to your friend. You must go to the lake just over the rise and store up on water. Princess Charity is depending on you. You must hurry because she is in trouble.

Meanwhile Michael and Marrissa started on their way again, they saw wizard hill, they were stunned by the size of the hill. They rested for awhile, and then started on their way again. They came to the base of the hill and tried to decide what would be the easiest way over, then they started over the hill. As the sky turned rosy pink, Michael and Marrissa were very tired, so they lay down to rest for the night. They figured to get an early start in the morning. So they slept the night and dreamed of their friends and what kind of trouble, their friends were in. They really wanted to help Barthalamew and Princess Charity. Marrissa started crying and sobbing about something.

Michael asked," Marrissa, what is the matter with you?"

Marrissa answered," I am afraid that we will never see our friends again."

The next morning Michael and Marrissa heard the sound of wings, it was a bunch of dragons, so they climbed back up to the spot where they couldn't be seen. They listened as the dragons came closer. Soon the dragons were close enough so they could be heard clearly, they were plotting to make one of them look like Barthalamew and create havoc in all the villages everywhere. Suddenly there was a golden eagle sitting beside them and they told the eagle what was going on and told him to find Barthalamew and tell him. The dragons finished their meeting and they all flew off to do whatever they wanted. Finally Marrissa and Michael came down off the hill and started on their way.

Barthalamew started on his way, he walked across the rise, and for a long way. He came to the lake and filled up on water and started across the desert. As he walked across the desert, he started to get hot and he had to find some shade, he sat down for a rest for a little while. Barthalamew had a strange feeling that someone was following him, but he shook it off. Finally he started on his way still thinking about who would be following him.

Meanwhile at the castle the dragons had returned and Thaldar was telling Zaldar about their plan.

Thaldar asked," Zaldar, could you make a potion or cast a spell to make one of us look like the dragon from the humans kingdom.

Zaldar answered," I will see what I can come up with for you."   So Zaldar went to his room and took some books off the shelf, he started flipping through a green book called, Potions for Changing. After awhile he picked up a purple book, Spells to Change anything. Soon he was writing something down on a piece of paper. Zaldar needed a few things so he made a list and sent Thaldar to find what was needed. The list read: grass from wizard hill, sand from the desert, leaves and bark of an oak tree, fresh water, moss from the river and a scale of a golden dragon. Thaldar took off to go find these things.

Meanwhile Barthalamew was getting very tired of walking and was very hot so Barthalamew found a place in the shade of a sand hill to rest for awhile. He lay down and went to sleep and started dreaming about Galdar. Galdar told Barthalamew what he, Galdar had been told. Barthalamew woke with a start, he tried to move but he was so tired he just couldn't move. So he settled back for a while longer.

Michael and Marrissa finally came to the lake and quite a little water and rested for awhile, soon they were on their way across the desert. It was very hot and the two little dragons were very tired. Soon they had to find shade, because Michael had to take care of Marrissa. Finally they found some shade under a bush and rested again, this was going to take longer than planned.

Marrissa said," Michael are you sure that we're alright out here?"

Michael said," We will be alright if we are very careful. Please don't get discouraged about it."

Marrissa asked," Do you think that Princess Charity and Barthalamew are alright?"

Michael answered," Yes, I believe that they are alright, but I am sure that Princess Charity is in some trouble."

Thaldar was in the forest getting the things that Zaldar needed. He was having some of the things on the list, but being a stubborn dragon, he kept trying. After what seemed like hours, he finally had everything except the sand from the desert and the scale of a golden dragon. Finally Thaldar started toward the desert, he came to the lake and decided to take a rest.

Barthalamew had started to walk again and he moved more slowly now. After quite awhile he came to the entrance of the cave and it was starting to get dark, so he climbed up about halfway to a ledge and settled down for the night. On the ledge outside the cave, Barthalamew was asleep and soon he was dreaming. He saw Galdar in his dream and Galdar told Barthalamew where to find Princess Charity and what was being planned. He also tried to get Barthalamew to go back. So Barthalamew planned a way to get in and save Princess Charity.

Back on the desert Michael and Marrissa settled into the cool area by the sand hill. Soon they spotted something out on the desert. As it got closer they saw that it was a dragon, so they turned invisible so they couldn't be seen. Thaldar collected the sand. Marrissa bumped a bush and it rattled, Thaldar turned around and looked in their direction, and saw nothing, so he went on about his business. Michael and Marrissa settled down for the night. Soon Thaldar was at the cave, and he gave Zaldar all the things that he had found.

Zaldar said," Everything is here except the scale of a golden dragon."

Thaldar said," There is only one golden dragon and he is friends with the humans.

Zaldar said," Tomorrow I want you to find that dragon and get me a scale."

Thaldar said," Yes, master Zaldar." Princess Charity heard everything, she had to figure out a way to get a message to Barthalamew, all of a sudden she saw a small gray mouse, she whispered to the mouse to find Barthalamew, a golden dragon and tell him what was happening. So the mouse took off and disappeared.

Soon all was quiet in the cave and Princess Charity settled down for the night.

Michael and Marrissa were sleeping in the desert, soon Galdar appeared to them and told them that they could help by getting caught. Then they could help trap the bunch of dragons and their master wizard. So they planned their way to get caught. Soon it was morning and they put their plan into motion, they started by walking and then Marrissa pretended that she hurt herself so that they would be caught. Soon Thaldar appeared from the sky. Then he landed beside the two little dragons, he grabbed them up and carried them back to the cave. He showed Zaldar what he had found on the desert.

Zaldar asked," What are you two young dragons doing on the desert all by yourselves?" Neither Michael or Marrissa answered him so Zaldar sprinkled some powder on Marrissa and she fell asleep.

Soon Barthalamew woke to the sound of the mouse telling him what was going on, then he started down off the ledge and caught a scale on the ledge, not realizing he had lost a scale he went on his way. Now he needed a way into this place to help his friend. All of a sudden he heard something coming and turned invisible. Thaldar came out and started looking for something. The sunlight caught on the scale. Thaldar spotted it and flew to where it was, he grabbed it and took off with it. He, Thaldar, took the scale to Zaldar, who finished his potion and changed Thaldar's brother to look like Barthalamew. They sent him to a small village and he destroyed at least half of it, then he headed for another village. By now Barthalamew was inside the cave, when he heard Zaldar tell Princess Charity and Michael about what he did. He told them the only way to change the out come of what was going to happen, was for the three dragons to forget their human friends and come live at dragon land. But Michael shouted," I will never forget my wonderful human friends and live in an awful place like this!"

Zaldar said," I will get you all to change for me and you can't stop me." Soon Barthalamew still invisible found a place to hide. Galdar came to him and told him that there was a dragon that looked like him destroying the villages. You must get to Zaldar's room and mix this potion, he will have everything in there, Galdar also explained the potion. So Barthalamew turning invisible, he slipped quietly into Zaldar's room and made the potion. Still invisible he sneaked back to the door and took off. Barthalamew flew because it is faster than walking, he flew all around and did not see the other dragon. So he went back to the cave, after returning to the cave, he turned invisible and went to set his friends free. Zaldar was busy in his room and couldn't hear what was going on in the other room. Barthalamew untied Princess Charity and told Michael to take the girls out of the cave and head for home.

Michael said," I can't carry Marrissa and she is asleep."

Barthalamew said," I will carry her to a safe place and you all can stay there until I get back." He took them to the ledge outside the cave and told Michael to stay on guard until he returned.

Finally Barthalamew went back into the cave and into the central room where he saw a beautiful gold and crystal scepter, he decided that it should go to the king, so he took hold of it and pulled it out of the rock that it was in. Soon he had it and was on his way again. Leaving the cave, he flew over the area again and finally found the other dragon and he flew over pouring the potion on the other dragon. The dragon changed back to the evil dragon, and said," I owe you a favor because you saved me."

Barthalamew said," I need the potion that will wake my fine little friend."

The other dragon said," How did this happen to your friend?"

Barthalamew answered," A wizard named, Zaldar did it to her."

The other dragon said," I will help you get the potion to wake your friend." So they started off for the cave.

At the cave Zaldar had an idea and a powder that would make the dragons forget their human friends. He was waiting for the arrival of Barthalamew. When Barthalamew arrived, Zaldar blew the powder on Barthalamew and almost immediately Barthalamew forgot about his human friends and all his dragon friends. Meanwhile outside Princess Charity and the dragons were still on the ledge waiting for Barthalamew to come back. But when he didn't come back, Princess Charity started to get worried about him. She started to sob, but Michael tried to comfort her, by now it was starting to get dark. So they settled in for a long night. While they were asleep Michael had a dream about Galdar, who told him what happened to Barthalamew, and how to help Barthalamew. Then he told him, he would see him in the morning.

In the cave all the dragons and Zaldar were talking about how they could capture the other dragons. Even Barthalamew was talking about it. Finally they fell asleep, while asleep Barthalamew had a dream about Galdar, but he couldn't remember who he was. So it was useless for him to try any longer. So Galdar went away and found the princess and the little dragons in their dreams. Galdar tells Michael and Princess Charity how to get away and save Barthalamew.

The next morning Michael and Princess Charity decided on a plan to get Barthalamew back to his old self, so Princess Charity gathered the items for the powder. Soon everything was ready, now all they needed to do was to get Barthalamew to come outside the cave. So Michael said," I will go in after Barthalamew and bring him out." Then Michael disappeared inside, soon Charity was feeling a little worried. In the cave Michael found the powder to wake Marrissa, he grabbed it and started out to get Barthalamew to follow him. Just then he heard a noise like someone stumbling. Then he saw Barthalamew, so he, Michael jumped out of his hiding spot and yelled. Finally he got Barthalamew to follow him, Michael headed for the cave entrance with Barthalamew right on his tail. As soon as Barthalamew came through the cave opening, Princess Charity threw the powder on Barthalamew and poof, he was himself again. After that they hurried to wake Marrissa , then they pushed a very large boulder down and blocked the opening. Then they left for home. They traveled across the desert and rested the night at the base of the wizard hill.

The next morning they flew over the hill and continued on their journey home by the time it started getting dark, they were finally coming to the kingdom. When they arrived they told everyone about the desert dragon land. Everyone was very happy that Barthalamew, Princess Charity, Michael and Marrissa were alright.

Barthalamew's Quest for a Golden Fleece

On a very hot August day, when the sun was high, Barthalamew was at his cave, when one of the king's men came and told him that the king needed him for a very special quest. Barthalamew went to the king and was told what he was suppose to do. After King Fredrick finished explaining, Barthalamew set off on his way. Barthalamew traveled for awhile and stopped to have a meal, after which he started on his way again.

In a small village not far from where Barthalamew was at, there was trouble and were in need of help. So Barthalamew stopped to help, the villagers were putting up a very large building and were having trouble, so he helped and they gave him a bottle of perfume. He put it in a pouch, then he said goodbye and left the village and went on his way, as he went on he started to travel a bit slower. He decided to go slower so he would not get as tired. Finally he came to a spot to rest, he fell asleep quickly.

The next morning Barthalamew started off once more, soon he was traveling through a forest and soon he came to an opening where he met a unicorn. The unicorn's name is, Starbright. At first Starbright was scared of Barthalamew, but finally they became friends. Soon Starbright and Barthalamew are on their way again. They started through the mountains, for several days, finally they stopped at a village called, Kalmira, where a young child, of six was very lost and lonely. She was in trouble and needed help, so Barthalamew and Starbright helped her find her way home, where they were rewarded with a large candle. Barthalamew put it in the pouch with the perfume. Then they were on their way again. Soon they came to the cave of diamonds. Barthalamew entered and found a place to sleep and then he called Starbright to his side, then they went to sleep.

In the morning they were on their way once more, as they traveled on they came to a village. In the village the gentiles welcome them. While they were in the village they helped many people with different things, each person gave them a different item. They received a gold coin, a small carving, a piece of trim and a silver goblet, which Bartholomew put in the pouch with the candle and the perfume. Then they left and were on the road again. Soon they traveled to a kingdom called Sharitona and in this kingdom was a pretty princess named, Katalina, she was fourteen years old, with dark brown hair and blue eyes. She was a very spirited young lady. Katalina saw the dragon and the unicorn. She went to them and asked," Who are you and where do you come from?"

Barthalamew answered," I am, Barthalamew and this is my friend Starbright. We are from Kalzara. We are on a quest for a golden fleece, can you help us find it?"

Katalina said," I am not able to help, but I know someone that can help you. Stay here and I will bring him back." So Barthalamew and Starbright waited for a long time, finally Katalina came back with a scorcer named Turlin. Turlin tells Barthalamew, he must travel through another stretch of mountains, then you will come to a large, dark, dusty, musty smelling cave, then he disappeared. Katalina told the travelers goodbye and God be with you. Before they left Barthalamew gave her the bottle of perfume. She excepted the gift, then Barthalamew and Starbright were on the road again.

After awhile Barthalamew and Starbright stopped and Barthalamew laid down to rest. While he was sleeping someone came and took Starbright. When Barthalamew woke up he thought that Starbright had gone for a walk. When he couldn't find her, he got upset, so he decided to fly over the land for awhile. Soon he spotted a strange little hut, Barthalamew flew in for a closer look. He found Starbright tied up in a stall. Barthalamew let her loose, but he got caught by a young man named, Waleron, he was a mean young man. Barthalamew said," I am here to rescue my friend."

Waleron said," Then you will have to take the consequence for freeing the unicorn." Then he tried to grab Barthalamew, but missed. Barthalamew was to fast, he moved so fast that Waleron could not catch him. Waleron was confused by this and fell to the ground. After he regained his balance, he chased Barthalamew for awhile, then he gave up. Starbright followed Barthalamew and then they were on their way toward the mountains and they moved very slowly because it was very hot. After awhile they stopped and rested for awhile, soon they came upon a small hut. This hut was practically falling down, being curious Barthalamew looked in. He saw a table in the center of the room. To the left is a bed and a make-shift stand. Across the room was a cupboard and a bunch of dishes. At the back of the hut was a fire pit. Barthalamew and Starbright didn't see anything that would help them, so they went on their way once more. As they travel they watch everything, Starbright spotted something in the underbrush. Barthalamew watched for a moment and he saw it as well. It was a little child of about six years of age, he seemed to be lost, but he also seemed to be looking for something.

Barthalamew asked," What are you looking for? Would you like some help, my friend and I would be glad to help."

The little boy named, Tomlin said," I could really use some help finding my dog, he ran away and I got lost trying to find him."

Barthalamew and Starbright helped Tomlin look for his dog and his home. When they returned Tomlin and his dog home, Tomlin's father Baron Thedius rewarded Barthalamew with a map, twenty gold pieces and two bottles of fine perfume. Into the pouch they did go, and they were on their way once more.

Barthalamew followed the map to yet another cave, Barthalamew and Starbright went in and started weaving around through the tunnels. Soon they came to a central room, in the center of the room was a golden fleece. Barthalamew traded the twenty gold pieces for the golden fleece, after exchanging the gold for the fleece, they, Barthalamew and Starbright finally started home. The duo traveled back through the mountains and the villages to return to Kalzara. They traveled for a long time, finally they stopped for the night.

The next morning was cloudy and cool so Barthalamew and Starbright traveled faster so they got further than when it was hot. They traveled for about an hour and someone snagged the pouch with all the stuff. Barthalamew and Starbright chased the person and finally caught him. He was a troll and wanted a friend. Well Barthalamew told the troll that he would be his friend, but he needed to give back the pouch.

Barthalamew said," I will be your friend, but I need to get back to Kalzara."

The troll said," My name is, Edward and I wish to have a friend. I am sorry I took your pouch."

Barthalamew said," To take someone else's stuff will not help you make any friends."

Edward said," Would you have room for one more in your little band?"

Barthalamew said," Of course we will make room for one more."

So on the trio traveled, after four more days the trio finally got to the Kingdom of Kalzara. First Barthalamew gave out the gifts he had. He gave Princess Charity a bottle of perfume, he gave Queen Isabella the other bottle of perfume and the trim, King Fredrick receives the silver goblet and the golden fleece, and Sir Currado receives the small wood carving. Finally Barthalamew went to his cave to dream about his next adventure. He dreamed of a very large ice castle and a purple dragon.

Barthalamew's Adventure to the Ice Castle

One nice day in the Kingdom of Kalzara, Princess Charity and Prince Theodore were in the garden playing with Michael and Marrissa. When Queen Isabella comes to the garden and tells the children and the little dragons the good news.

Queen Isabella said," Charity, you are going to be a big sister. I am going to have a baby."

Charity said," You are going to have a baby, how awesome I really want a sister or brother."

Then she asks to go tell Barthalamew, he mother gives her permission to go. So Princess Charity, Prince Theodore, Michael and Marrissa head out to go see Barthalamew and tell him the good news. They arrive at his cave, but he is not there. He was on his way to find Michael and Marrissa. So Princess Charity suggests that they go back through the forest as they walk through the forest they see a strange person there. Somehow the little dragons get separated from Princess Charity and Prince Theodore. They get headed in the wrong direction, then they ran into the strange person and almost knocked him down. He grabs Michael and Marrissa and takes them to the

Ice castle. The man puts Michael and Marrissa in the dungeon, while in the dungeon, they meet a purple dragon named, Gabby. Gabby tells them that she has been trapped here for two weeks. Gabby asks," Can you help me get out of here?"

Michael said," We have no idea how to get out of here either."

Marrissa starts to sob," I want my friends, Princess Charity, Prince Theodore and Barthalamew to come save us."

Back in the forest Princess Charity and Prince Theodore realize that the little dragons were gone. They started looking for Michael and Marrissa, with no luck. While looking for the little dragons they meet up with Barthalamew, they tell Barthalamew what happened and wanted him to see if he could find them. Barthalamew told them, that he would find them. So off he flew, after a very long time Barthalamew landed and walked for a long way. Still no sign of the little dragons. A couple of hours go by and still no sign of the little dragons, so he went back to the place he left Princess Charity and Prince Theodore, then they all went back to the castle and told King Fredrick and Queen Isabella what had happened to the little dragons.

Meanwhile at the Ice Castle Michael, Marrissa and Gabby were trying to figure out a way so they could go home. Gabby is looking really very sad and Marrissa wanted to know why she was so sad.

Marrissa asked," How come you are so sad, Gabby?"

Gabby answered," I have no home to go to, so when I leave here, I will end up wandering from place to place."

Michael said," We will make sure you have a home when we leave here. We will ask our human friends if you can live with us."

Gabby said," You live with humans, humans kill dragons. No human will ever be my friend." Then she started to scream for no reason at all. She continued to scream for the longest time. Finally she quit screaming and then she sat in the corner and cried. Marrissa tried to comfort her and assure her that humans could be really nice. Before long the strange man came to the dungeon and grabbed Gabby and took her somewhere.

He took Gabby up to a bedroom and left her there. Soon a little girl came in and started pulling Gabby's tail. Gabby didn't like it so she snapped at the child. The child let out with a howl that could be heard all over the kingdom. Then the strange man came in and grabbed Gabby and took her into another room where he hit her with a strap made of heavy leather, then he took her back to the dungeon, then he took Marrissa and left. He took Marrissa into the child's room and the little girl started hitting Marrissa and pulling her tail. Marrissa tried to talk to her, but she wouldn't listen. So Marrissa slapped her with her tail, the girl let out a scream that scared Marrissa. The man came in and took Marrissa into another room and slapped her with the heavy leather strap and then tied her to a device on the wall and hit her some more. Then he took her back to the dungeon and put her with the other two.

King Fredrick and Queen Isabella had just set up a search party for the little dragons. The search party searched and searched, but no sign of the little dragons anywhere. They searched everyday for at least a week and still never found the two dragons. Barthalamew searched the whole kingdom and could find no sign of the two dragons. Everyone was very worried about the little dragons. No one gave up on finding them. Queen Isabella was so worried about the little dragons that she got sick and had to stay in bed. She was told not to get up for anything, except to go to the bathroom. So she lay in bed bored out of her gourd.

The dungeon was very cold and damp, Michael, Marrissa and Gabby were all miserable. The man came to the dungeon and told them if they would get along with the Ice Princess they wouldn't get hit anymore and he would leave them alone. The dragons refused the offer to try to get along with that evil little girl. So it went on day after day. No one in the castle here cared for the dragons or how they were treated. The three little dragons wanted to go home. They really tied to figure out how they could get out of this situation .

At the castle King Fredrick checked on Queen Isabella and made sure she was alright. Then he went to see how the search for the little dragons was going. King Fredrick told the group to keep looking there has to be something that can lead us to the little dragons. They looked again where they thought the little dragons disappeared, they searched under every bit of underbrush and anywhere that there could be a clue. Suddenly Sir Currado spotted something and picked it up a hair clip.

At the Ice Castle, Marrissa reminds Michael that he has teleportation powers. So Michael teleports out of the ice castle dungeon, and flies to the kingdom of Kalzara and finds Sir Currado and tells him where to find the girls. Then Michael flies back to the ice castle and teleports back into the dungeon, before the strange man came. The man finally figured out that the little dragons were never going to like the Ice Princess. So he finally quit taking the girls to her room, it was very hard for Michael not to attack the strange man. As the man left Michael told the girls that King Fredrick's knights were coming to get them. They head out to see if you can find the little dragons and bring them back. So they traveled for several days to get to where Michael told them that they were being held. The knights came to a place in the mountains that they could not get through. So they had to find a different route through the mountains.

Michael, Marrissa and Gabby were still trying to figure out how to get away. The strange man came and took the three dragons to appear in front of the Ice Queen because they refused to get along with the Ice Princess. The Ice Queen told them that if they would get along and play with her daughter that, she wouldn't put them back in the dungeon. The little dragons told her that they would never get along with that spoiled child. Gabby started to cry and fuss. Michael tried to get her to stop, the more he tried to stop her the worse she got. So the Ice Queen had the man ,put them back in the dungeon. Back in the dungeon Michael, Marrissa and Gabby huddled close together for warmth, because it was so cold down there. Day after day the man came and took the little dragons in front of the Queen, and every day the dragons gave the same reason when she would ask them to be friends with her daughter. Day after day they would end up back In the dungeon. Gabby said," Now you see why I don't like humans."

Michael said," But all humans aren't bad people, just some of them."

Marrissa said," Our humans are very nice and would never hurt any dragon." So Gabby decided that when they left here, that she would try to live with their humans.

In the mountains the knights became lost and could not remember which way to go to get to the ice castle. They travel for several more days then they came to a maze, they had to figure out how to get through the maze. The knights couldn't seem to figure out how to get through. So they kept trying to figure it out, finally after quite awhile they got a bit further. It still took the knights a really long time to get anywhere in the maze.

The little dragons really want to get away from this terrible place and show Gabby that all people aren't bad. They play games to keep their minds off the situation that they are in. The little dragons are beginning to wonder if anyone will ever save them. Gabby said," I told you humans couldn't be trusted." Then she proceeded to throw a temper fit. So Michael and Marrissa decided that if she wouldn't believe her they would have to show her. Michael teleported out of the dungeon and flew to find Sir Currado and his group. He found them in the maze where they had been lost for two days. He told them that they need to hurry to get them out. He told them that they, the little dragons were in trouble because they wouldn't do what the Ice Queen wanted. " So would you hurry?" asked Michael.

Sir Currado said," We will get there as soon as we can, alright." So Michael went back to the ice dungeon.

In the dungeon Gabby was catching a cold and was getting very sick. Marrissa and Michael did everything they could to help keep her happy. Michael hoped that Sir Currado and the knights come soon. Michael and Marrissa took turns caring for Gabby, while they waited for the knights to come save them. Finally they decided that they had to do something to get Gabby out of here and get her to someone that could help her get better. So Michael tried to teleport her outside, but it didn't work. So they just kept doing what they were to keep going.

Meanwhile the knights finally got through the maze and started toward the castle. Where they meet up with a very large Ice Dragon, who would not let them pass. So they had to fight the Ice Dragon, because they knew they had to save the little dragons. So several of the knights started using their swords and hitting the dragon but the swords only bounced off the ice. So they made a plan that some of the knights would keep the dragon busy while the rest went to save the little dragons. So some of the knights kept hitting the dragon and then Sir Currado and some other knights went in after the little dragons. Then Sir Currado and his men got caught by one of the guards. They were taken to the Ice Queen where they were told that the three little dragons were never going to leave. Sir Currado reminded her who gave her this land in the first place. Then she told him," You will never have the little dragons back because they do not trust humans anymore.

In the dungeon Michael has started to dig a tunnel to get the girls out. It was a slow process, because he couldn't blow fire for very long at a time. He kept working on the tunnel, as long as no one was coming.

Marrissa kept caring for Gabby to try to make her feel better. The only way that she would get better was to get her out of here. Michael was almost through when the man came and grabbed him and took him to the Queen, who told the man to put him in the special room, that no dragon could escape from. So the man did what she told him to. Then he went back to his room. The knights told her that they would get those little dragons out of here somehow. She had her guards tie the knights up and lock them in another cell in the dungeon. After awhile Sir Currado got free and then untied the other knights and they found a bunch of dry wood and started a fire by the door which melted, so they found the two girl dragons and went to find Michael. They finally found Michael and got him free. Then they set up a distraction and finally got the little dragons out. The little dragons were so worn out that they could hardly walk. Just by luck Bartholomew had figured out where they were and swooped down and everyone got on so they could go home. Barthalamew asked," Who is this pretty little dragon?"

Michael said," This is our new friend Gabby, the Ice Queen had her captured to become friends with the Ice Princess. But when it didn't work, she had Marrissa and I captured for the same reason."

Marrissa said," She doesn't trust humans, because she was hit with a leather strap over and over, so she trusts no humans." Barthalamew flew to a valley where it was a bit warmer. He knew they had to get Gabby back to the castle so they could get her well. But it would be slow going carrying everyone.

At the ice castle the Queen was furious at her men for letting the little dragons get away. But she knew that she could not leave the castle or she would be no more. So she sent ten of her men to go find the little dragons. Search as they may they could not find the little dragons anywhere. The men went back to the ice castle and told the Ice Queen that they could not find them anywhere. She told them to go keep looking, for a little dragon that could become a playmate for the Ice Princess. So they went to see what they could do. They looked and looked with no luck at all. Then they had the idea to go to other kingdoms.

Meanwhile Barthalamew had suggested that he take Marrissa and Gabby to the castle at Caldara and get Gabby some help. Then he would come back and get the rest of the men and Michael. Everyone decided that would be the best, because they didn't want Gabby to get any worse than she already was. So Marrissa got on Barthalamew and Sir Currado handed Gabby to her, then Barthalamew took off for the castle. They arrive at the castle and land, Princess Charity sees Barthalamew and ran to him. She said," Who is this little dragon?"

Marrissa answered," This is Gabby, she was a prisoner of the Ice Queen for a long time. She is very scared of humans, so be careful not to scare her worse."

Barthalamew said," King Fredrick, this little dragon is very sick and needs medicine, can you help her."

King Fredrick said," I will do what I can for her. Seems to me she has a bad cold." Just then he heard a scream from upstairs. He went to see if Queen Isabella was alright. She was in pain and King Fredrick called for her Lady to attend to her. Then he went down to see what he could do for the little dragon. Gabby was awake a little, she shied away from the King. He told that he would not hurt her, he only wanted to help her. So she let him touch her and give her some medicine to help her get better.

In the meantime Barthalamew went after the others. He flew back to where he had left the rest of the knights and Michael. Michael asked," How is my little friend, Gabby?"

Barthalamew said," She is under the watchful eye of the King and Princess Charity, she will get better now.

Michael said," I want to get home so I can help care for her."

Barthalamew said," Well then let's get going, so we can get back, it is starting to get dark." So everyone got on Barthalamew and they headed home to the castle. When they arrived at the castle there was all kinds of things going on. Princess Charity and Marrissa were taking care of Gabby. The King was upstairs with the Queen. Everyone was hurrying and scurrying around some with blankets, some with large pots of hot water and others were cleaning the nursery. Before long everyone heard crying, the baby was here. For a whole week Marrissa kept watch over Gabby. Princess

Charity helped, when Gabby was well, she finally realized that all humans weren't bad.

As time goes by Gabby grows bigger and stronger. Michael and Marrissa start teaching her how to hunt for food and other dragon things. If Gabby didn't get what she wanted she would start to cry and scream and throw temper tantrums to get what she wanted. King Fredrick really didn't like the way she was acting so he decided that Barthalamew could train her to understand that she can't always get what she wants. At the same time the baby Prince was growing like crazy, he really liked playing with the dragons. Barthalmew, Michael, Marrissa and Gabby all liked to help with the baby. They named the baby , Jeremy , the little one was so cute. He had medium brown hair and blue eyes. The dragons were very protective of Prince Jeremy.

A couple of months later Princess Charity wanted to go on an adventure. Barthalamew was getting bored with having no adventures so he went to see Princess Charity, who was helping her mother with Prince Jeremy. The three little dragons were playing in the garden. Prince Theodore came over to see Princess Charity and Prince Jeremy. They all lived in the kingdom happily from then on. Cover design.